Leena Parkkinen

Translated by Ruth Urbom

Illustrated by Katja Wehner

Boje

COW BELLE BEAUTY QUEEN

Published 2013 by Little Island

7 Kenilworth Park, Dublin 6W, Ireland

www.littleisland.ie

First published as *Miss Milky Ray* by Teos in Helsinki in 2011

Published by agreement with Stilton Literary Agency, Finland.

Copyright © Leena Parkkinen 2011

Translation copyright © Ruth Urbom 2013

Illustrations by Katja Wehner

© 2013 Boje Verlag in the Bastei Lübbe GmbH & Co. KG

The author and translator have asserted their moral rights.

ISBN Paperback 978-1-908195-31-9

ISBN ePub 978-1-908195-81-4

ISBN mobi 978-1-908195-82-1

British Library Cataloguing Data.

A CIP catalogue record for this book is available from the British Library.

Cover design by Oldtown Graphic Design; illustration by Katja Wehner.

Typeset in PNM Caecilia Light by Oldtown Graphic Design.

Printed in Germany by CPI – Ebner & Spiegel, Ulm.

Little Island receives financial assistance from
The Arts Council (An Chomhairle Ealaíon), Dublin, Ireland.

This work has been published with the financial assistance of
FILI– Finnish Literature Exchange.

The publisher acknowledges the financial assistance of
Ireland Literature Exchange (translation fund), Dublin, Ireland.
www.irelandliterature.com | info@irelandliterature.com

10 9 8 7 6 5 4 3 2 1

Milena was brushing her teeth in front of the bathroom mirror. She had to do it carefully, because otherwise the stitches in her tongue might get torn. A month ago, Milena had been in an accident where two cars drove – bam! – straight into each other. The cars split in two like melons, and Milena had got such a fright she'd bitten right through her tongue. There had been a lot of blood. Almost as if Milena had been dipped in ketchup.

Other than that, she was in excellent health. As healthy as any ordinary eight-year-old could be, even though she had stitches going across her tongue, just like a patchwork quilt. Sometimes she imagined she was a patchwork herself.

A machine made up of various bits of skin and organs that did the things it was supposed to do (such as brushing its teeth right now), and not a girl called Milena at all.

There were just three puffs to go before bed. Milena had to make the most of them, because her mum timed them with a stopwatch. She would have thought that grown-ups, who didn't get told to brush their teeth and get under the covers, would KNOW how to have fun doing important things, but no. (Milena often thought things to herself in capital letters. Especially because she knew her mum hated them.)

Suddenly Milena heard splashing noises coming from the bath. She pricked up her ears and froze for a moment. The plughole squelched as if a massive submarine were swimming in the bath. *Get ready for a fight*, Milena thought to herself.

She crept cautiously over to the shower curtain and raised her toothbrush. Even an idiot knows that bogeymen are really scaredy-cats, despite their fierce looks, and that a quick attack is the best defence against them. With a swift movement, Milena took hold of one corner of the shower curtain and pulled it aside.

There was a cow in the bath. It was scrubbing its back with the loo brush, and there were soap bubbles coming out of its nostrils.

'Would you put the curtain back, please?' said the cow. 'My skin can't take the draught.'

Milena opened her mouth, but all her best smart remarks had deserted her. She pulled the shower curtain closed again, climbed up and sat on the toilet lid, tucking her feet underneath her. She counted to ten and opened the curtain a tiny bit.

The cow was lounging in the bath. It didn't even bother to look embarrassed. Instead, it was singing 'Row, row, row your boat' out of tune.

'Milena!' Milena's mum called out from downstairs. 'Have you got tummy-ache or something? Why are you moaning and groaning?'

Milena could hear the theme tune to WestEnders, her mum's favourite soap, in the background. That meant Mum wouldn't bother her for half an hour. Milena would have the situation sorted by then. It was no use getting grown-ups mixed up in anything. They always started offering you vitamin pills and chatting to people in white coats.

'Everything'th fine,' she called back. She had a slight lisp because it hurt to speak.

'Who was that?' the cow asked.

'That'th my mum.'

'Mums don't seem to know much about music,' the cow said. 'But what can you expect from humans, when they've got noses like that?'

'Notheth?' Milena asked. She was starting to sense that this encounter could have gone a lot more smoothly all round.

'Yuck,' said the cow. 'Human noses. I can't stand them.'

'Why'th that?' Milena asked, covering her own nose with the palm of her hand.

'They look just like caterpillar holes,' said the cow. 'A little bump with two hollows in it. I half-expect something white and slimy to come slithering out at any moment. But then again,' the cow continued, 'I suppose you can't expect everyone to have as fine a muzzle as this.'

Milena thought the cow looked a bit self-important as she massaged her face with the brush.

'Do you know that'th a toilet bruth? It'th for cleaning the loo.'

'Oh?' said the cow. 'Aren't your loos clean?'

'Erm, never mind,' Milena snorted. The cow was really and truly starting to get her goat. 'Tell me, are you thome kind of bogeyman?'

'A bogeyman!' the cow snorted, raising its muzzle. 'I'm a first-class Ayrshire: 600 kilos, not including my horns.'

'You look much slimmer than that,' said Milena. She wondered whether Ayrshire was a word in some bogeyman language.

'I'm sure I don't,' the cow sniffed. 'No one in our family line ever weighed less than 520 kilos. Not even my little sister Donatella, who's a Pirkkala piebald on her father's side. But we don't talk about that. A cow has to accept her family, even when some of them are real beasts.' As the cow guffawed at her own wit, she got soap in her eyes and had to rinse it out.

'But what are you doing in MY bath?' Milena asked.

'Having a bath,' the cow replied. 'My dear little calf, you don't appear to be particularly bright. And it's not terribly pretty to sit there with your mouth gaping open, but then again, you human calves aren't raised all that well. What can one expect from the sort of people who don't start each morning with some nourishing hay stew and calcium powder? No wonder your heads stay so small.'

The cow got out of the bath and wrapped a red striped towel around its horns.

'You can't tell how smart someone is from how big they are,' Milena maintained.

'Now now, little calf. Are you claiming you're dumber than a hamster? My name is Semi-Skimmed Tetra Pak,' the cow said. 'You could at least be civilised enough to introduce yourself.'

'My name ith Milena.'

'You humans speak with a strange accent. If you were a cow, I'd say you had a lisp.'

'You're the one with a lithp,' Milena snapped illogically.

Then she explained about her tongue and all about the accident and why her mum spent all day just lying on the sofa eating ice cream. And why they'd rented this house for the whole summer. And how Milena was worried about whether she'd ever learn to speak normally. Or would she spend the rest of her life as an outcast who couldn't even spell the word 'squirm' without lisping?

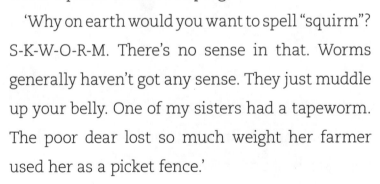

'Why on earth would you want to spell "squirm"? S-K-W-O-R-M. There's no sense in that. Worms generally haven't got any sense. They just muddle up your belly. One of my sisters had a tapeworm. The poor dear lost so much weight her farmer used her as a picket fence.'

'That'th not how you thpell it.'

'You'll see,' Semi-Skimmed said. 'If I were you, I wouldn't worry too much about conversations with one-bellies. They're boring. You yourself haven't said much of interest in this conversation.'

'One-bellieth?'

'That's what we cows call you. Chewing the cud is associated with more mature thought processes.'

'But it'th not thpelt ETH-K-W-O-R-M. There'th a Q in it.'

'How do you know? Have you ever read a cow spelling book?'

'No.' Milena wanted to add that she hadn't even heard of such a thing until that very moment.

'Cow spelling books never use a Q in the middle of a word. We think it's vulgar.'

Semi-Skimmed drew out the last word, making her muzzle shudder. That made her look just like

Milena's Auntie Ulrika, who was very la-di-dah, as Mum said.

'MILENA!' Mum shouted from downstairs. 'Stop sploshing around in the water. Do you know how much it costs to heat water?'

'Shh,' Milena shushed the cow. 'If Mum thees you here, there'll be an awful racket.'

Milena had learnt that her mum got terribly upset around anything unusual. The other day Milena had brought home a lovely sleek grass snake that had a kind, longing expression. It seemed to be begging to be allowed to sleep on Milena's pillow and eat from the same bowl of breakfast cereal as she did. But when the snake wriggled its way out of Milena's pyjamas at breakfast and into her mum's bowl of yoghurt, Mum had leapt onto her chair and screamed with her hands over her ears. Milena had to take it back to the ditch that was its home.

Milena knew this cow business had to be sorted with the minimum of fuss – otherwise there'd be weeping and wailing all over again. You could always count on adults to make an awful lot of noise.

Semi-Skimmed wasn't interested in Milena's mum. She dried off the steamed-up bathroom mirror and inspected her eyelashes in it. Milena had to poke her in the side and explain twice why it was so important that her mum didn't find out about Semi-Skimmed. She put two pairs of

woollen socks that her granny had knitted onto the cow's hooves to soften her steps.

Downstairs the TV was blaring. The lovers in *WestEnders* seemed to be in the middle of a massive row, and Mum's eyes were glued to the screen.

One, two, three – Milena counted the steps to herself as she followed the cow downstairs. Then, all of a sudden, it happened: halfway down the staircase, Semi-Skimmed slipped. (Milena had to admit that maybe the woollen socks hadn't been the most brilliant idea.) *Whump, whump,* the cow bounced down the rest of the steps with her legs outstretched. Milena froze in terror. For a moment there was total silence. The feuding soap-opera characters just glared at each other.

'Milena,' Mum began. 'What on earth ...' Just at that moment, the main character in the soap said, 'But Gladys, I'm actually your brother,' and Mum's voice trailed off.

Semi-Skimmed staggered up off the floor and tiptoed over towards the front door. Her previous boastfulness was gone. Milena could see that she was as embarrassed as a fully grown cow could possibly be. Her tail hung limp and her horns were tilted. She slipped out the door so quickly that Milena started to think she'd imagined the whole thing.

The next morning there was a smell of fresh grass in the air. Milena had dreamt about the cow and how it chewed clover in a meadow. The dream felt real – Milena could almost hear Semi-Skimmed burping.

She ran downstairs, where her mum was squinting at the coffee maker. Milena switched the coffee maker on and dashed out the door. The meadow was empty. Milena checked everywhere – even in the ditch, although she knew that Semi-Skimmed wouldn't be able to hide in the knee-deep ditch, even if someone was threatening her with a vitamin injection.

Milena went back home, where she found her

mum staring at a full cup of coffee that had gone cold. Milena poured herself some coffee from the jug and filled the remaining two-thirds of her cup with milk. Normally she didn't really care for coffee, but nothing seemed to make sense this morning. What was so great about drinking this stuff?

After her third cup of coffee, Milena's mum snapped out of her trance and ordered Milena to go and brush her teeth. Brushing your teeth in the school holidays is ridiculous, but Milena didn't raise an objection. You just couldn't discuss anything sensible with Mum before lunch, like how they absolutely needed to get a trampoline for the garden if Mum expected Milena to get good marks in PE.

While she was brushing her teeth Milena checked in the bath just to make sure, but it was empty. She went into her room and jumped onto the bed.

'Ow,' came a noise from the bed. 'It's not terribly civilised to prod others with your hooves.'

20

'What are you doing in my bed?' Milena leapt to her feet and stared at the duvet, which bulged and rose into a shapeless form until the cow's muzzle poked out from underneath.

'Oh, did Goldilocks eat everyone's porridge? What do you think? I'm warming up. It's freezing outside, in case you hadn't noticed.' Semi-Skimmed's words were slightly muffled.

When she looked more closely, Milena could see biscuit crumbs on the cow's muzzle.

'We've got to stop meeting like this,' Milena said in a stern voice, just like the hunky man in *WestEnders*, but the cow didn't seem to hear her.

'Have you got any more of those chocolate-coated ones with pink sprinkles on top?'

'Yesterday you were saying how grass is so nutritious and beneficial for the brain,' Milena said.

'Grass is overrated. The right food for cows is chocolate biscuits. But we've got to discuss something important now. You're very prone to idle chitter-chatter. I suspect you haven't been raised properly,' Semi-Skimmed said.

'I've raised myself,' Milena replied, because she took the view that bringing up children was something that shouldn't be left to adults. Most of the time they were wrapped up in the mass media and something called 'meetings', which involved sitting in a little room eating pastries.

'You've got to help me,' Semi-Skimmed pleaded, taking a wrapper from under the duvet and handing it to Milena.

Milena stared at it. It looked like an ordinary chocolate-bar wrapper.

'This is my ticket to becoming the Princess of Meadowville,' said Semi-Skimmed, gazing at Milena with her moist cow eyes. Milena stared open-mouthed at her. 'You've got to help me win the Cow Belle Beauty Queen pageant.'

Milena thought this sounded ridiculous and sat down on the floor. She found the packet of biscuits, which Semi-Skimmed had nicked almost all of, and started munching as the cow spoke. The biscuits didn't taste as good without milk, but it would have felt wrong somehow to drink milk in the presence of a dairy cow.

Semi-Skimmed was talking so excitedly, it took Milena a while to understand what she was on about. But here's a brief summary: once every three years, the Milky Ray chocolate factory selected the prettiest cow in Meadowville. As well as the title of Cow Belle Beauty Queen (which all the cows craved), the winner would get her photo printed on every Milky Ray-bar wrapper during her three-year reign.

'The current title-holder is Hefty Hoofington, that old heifer. You wouldn't believe the way she's been swanning about, even though everyone knows her father's a Belgian blue.'

'Belgian blue?'

'They're supposed to be posh, but in fact they've got two bums. Inbred beasts.' Milena was about to ask about the bum thing, but Semi-Skimmed carried on with her commentary. Hefty and Semi-Skimmed were clearly old enemies, and they were related on their mothers' side.

'She wasn't raised in the same cowshed as me, but close,' Semi-Skimmed explained. Hefty had tormented her even when they were young calves. Dared her to eat poisonous buttercups, which upset all of Semi-Skimmed's stomachs. Egged her on to wade into a lake with a steep shoreline. Once she even shoved Semi-Skimmed against an electric fence and claimed it was an accident.

Even as a calf, Hefty had been big – a real bruiser – and chocolate brown. Cows like that can often have a hard time of it too.

'The truth is, I really do weigh only 500 kilos. I'm the smallest cow in my whole family,' Semi-Skimmed admitted, her muzzle drooping. 'I haven't got a chance.'

'Never mind,' Milena said, feeling sorry for the cow. 'I'll help you!'

Semi-Skimmed perked up. 'Really?' She charged over to hug Milena, but the girl jumped out of the way in the nick of time. Even a petite Ayrshire weighing several hundred kilos delivers a lot of force with a hug. Semi-Skimmed didn't seem to mind and just jumped up and down, making the floorboards in Milena's bedroom groan.

'First, you've got to tell me everything that's involved in the competition. Then we can draw up a training programme. I've watched enough films to know about all that stuff,' Milena explained.

The lakeside meadow was the safest place to practise. The shore was too muddy for swimming and the meadow was too remote for sunbathers. People had kept pigs there in the past, but now not even a single trotter-print remained in the soil. The only thing left was an old tumbledown fence from the pigpen.

'The toughest part is the talent competition,' Milena said. She had put on her best red tracksuit because she thought this session would require special effort. 'What are you thinking of doing for that?'

'Singing,' Semi-Skimmed answered. 'When I was just a calf I appeared in the dairy's summer stock production of *Annie, Chew Your Cud*. It was a huge success. Some of the meadow gang came to watch me from as far away as the edge of the forest, even though it was peak season for flies.'

To prove it, Semi-Skimmed let out a long bellow. Milena fell onto her bum in the sticky earth. The cow's voice sounded as if someone was skinning a rabbit and yodelling with a mouthful of peppermints. Through a megaphone.

Pleased with herself, Semi-Skimmed bobbed her head and shook out her legs as if she'd just been for a long run.

'Pretty impressive, eh?'

'Maybe we could think of something else. Just in case,' said Milena as she wiped the mud from her new tracksuit.

Every afternoon the following week, Milena and Semi-Skimmed met up in the lakeside meadow to do their exercise programme. They jumped over the fence, ran through car tyres and stretched their hindquarters until they creaked.

One evening a faint haze had already crept towards the lakeshore, heralding nightfall, as Semi-Skimmed danced the twist and skipped with a rope at the same time among the birch trees. She claimed the twist was the best way for a cow to keep her hooves in shape. Milena was concentrating on making garlands out of clover and daisies. Semi-Skimmed had told her that every cow in the competition wore a flower garland like that round her neck, but it was slow work making them.

Suddenly Milena noticed a shadow falling over her garland. Quickly, she turned round and saw three cows standing behind her. The one in the middle was absolutely enormous, as big as a bull and velvety chocolate brown. It was grinning, but its expression didn't look very friendly to Milena. The creature had huge horns and flaring nostrils. The other two were brownish-coloured

as well, but they had lighter patches on their backs. They were slightly smaller than the brown cow, but each of them seemed to be about twice as big as Semi-Skimmed.

Milena leapt to her feet. Semi-Skimmed hadn't noticed a thing. She was singing a little tune to herself and leaping about, making the ground shake.

'So, little calf-person,' said the brown cow – and

now Semi-Skimmed noticed her as well. Semi-Skimmed stopped so suddenly that she tripped over her skipping rope and flew backwards, landing on her rump. She tried to get back up but her hooves got tangled up in the rope and she fell down even harder.

'I see Skimmy's been learning to dance,' the brown cow said, mooing at her own joke.

'Hefty,' Semi-Skimmed muttered. Milena gave a little jump.

'How delightful that you've decided to take part in the competition too,' Hefty sneered. 'We girls decided to come and congratulate you. And I see you've found someone to play with,' she added, nodding in Milena's direction. She snatched the flower garland Milena had been working on from the ground and started chewing it. 'Really good snacks here. Your human's a bit odd-looking, but it doesn't make a half-bad garland.'

'Nobody wants to be around her, except some human,' one of the spotted cows mooed, and her friend sniggered.

'Now, now, girls,' said Hefty. 'Let's be nice. It makes you beautiful.'

'Thanks,' Semi-Skimmed muttered. Milena thought she looked as if she didn't know what to think.

'And even a tiny bit of beautification can only help a muzzle like that,' Hefty added. 'They ought to keep that sort away from the milking parlour, otherwise the milk will go sour.'

The trio came closer, pointing their horns at Semi-Skimmed, who stopped untangling her skipping rope to back away. The cows followed, shoving Semi-Skimmed forward.

'Stop it,' Milena shouted.

'Yeah, sure,' Hefty said as she tipped Semi-Skimmed over.

Semi-Skimmed fell right into a bed of nettles growing by the side of the pigpen fence.

'Yeeow, it stings,' Semi-Skimmed shrieked. The spotted cows burst out laughing.

'Let's go, girls,' said Hefty, wagging her tail in satisfaction. 'I think Skimmy's learnt her lesson.'

Once the cows had left, Milena went over to help Semi-Skimmed. Her head was drooping and she avoided making eye contact with Milena.

'Well, now you know what a pathetic coward I am,' she said.

Milena patted her. Just then, Milena noticed something and cried out. Semi-Skimmed's whole flank had broken out in thumbnail-sized red bumps.

'You look like you've got scarlet fever.'

'Nettle rash,' said Semi-Skimmed, trying to turn her head to look at her own back. 'I've been allergic to nettles ever since I was a calf. Hefty *knew* that. How on earth can I take part in the pageant in two days' time?'

'Quick, go for a swim,' said Milena. 'The water will help.'

Semi-Skimmed's eyelids were beginning to swell up. She staggered forward, half-blind, with Milena supporting her. The lakeshore sloped steeply, and soon the water was halfway up the cow's flanks. Milena's feet didn't reach the bottom, so she had to swim round Semi-Skimmed and splash water onto her back. The water was muddy, and in the end Semi-Skimmed was completely covered in a thick layer of brown sludge. Her eyes were streaming. All in all, she was a sorry sight.

Milena would have laughed if the situation hadn't been so serious. She had to lead the cow to the shore. Blobs of brown clay dripped off with each step.

'Did that help?' Milena asked.

'What does it look like?' Semi-Skimmed spluttered. If it had been anyone else, Milena would have said her voice sounded like she was crying.

As she stood still, the mud started to harden and flake off Semi-Skimmed's hide.

'You can imagine it's a mud pack,' said Milena.

'I'll pack some mud in your face pretty soon, you cheeky girl,' said Semi-Skimmed.

'We need to get you clean,' Milena said, remembering there was a garden hose in the shed. Fortunately her mum was indoors watching some programme about teenage vampires, so Milena managed to get Semi-Skimmed rinsed off fairly well. The bumps on her side had gone purple now.

'Maybe we can use some of Mum's foundation,' Milena suggested.

'That's a pig of an idea,' the cow grumbled. 'I'm not some laboratory test animal.'

'Once, Mum had a skin rash and she put some kind of cream on it. We could try that,' Milena suggested. 'But we need to wait until it gets dark. Mum doesn't spend much time in the garden, but even she might notice a 500-kilo cow galumphing around on her doorstep.'

Semi-Skimmed was feeling low. She didn't feel like resisting, so she just trudged along with her knees bent, dragging up the soil.

The expression on the woman's face at the chemist's was a sight to be seen when Milena asked her for 25 litres of cream for nettle rash. She was a refined lady with freckles who stood proudly in her white coat with a name badge on the front.

'D … do you mean you want a 25-gram tube of itch cream? Have you got a nasty rash, little girl?' the lady asked with a sympathetic expression that was downright sweet.

Milena frowned. 'No,' she replied, 'but thank you for asking. I've got some freckles on my tummy, but they're for decoration. Do you mean you only sell it in really large tubs? In that case, I'll take fifty litres. That'll be enough for the next-door neighbours too.'

'And just why do you need so much cream?' the lady asked.

'I'm planning to polish the car with it,' Milena said. She guessed it would not be wise to bring the cow into the conversation. 'It would be good to have enough to polish my shoes as well.'

The lady shook her head. 'We don't sell containers that big here.'

'Well, maybe I'll forget about the neighbours then. Let them get their own stupid goo. I'll take all the brands you've got.'

Milena tied the parcel with all the creams and tubes she'd bought onto the rack on the back of her bike, then pedalled home past the church and waited for evening to come.

Mum was downstairs watching a German detective programme where all the actors wore black leather jackets. From time to time Milena would go downstairs to get something: a glass of milk, an extra pillow or a cheese sandwich. She tried to peep in to see whether her mum was asleep yet. Usually she would doze off during the opening titles and not wake up until the programme was over, and then ask what had happened. But just now her mum was sitting on the sofa, worryingly alert, eating pistachios straight out of the packet.

'Aren't you getting sleepy?' Milena asked as her mother cheered on the German cop to nab the burglar.

'Have you got a dodgy tummy? What are you doing trotting down here all the time?' her mum

asked. 'Have you brushed your teeth yet?' she added, seeming to remember her role as a mother for a moment.

'I'm just getting a glass of warm milk,' Milena said cleverly. 'Would you like one too?'

Mum nodded, her eyes glued to the screen. Fifteen or twenty minutes after that glass of milk, loud snoring could be heard coming from the sofa.

Milena crept over to the front door and peeped out.

'Semi-Skimmed,' she whispered into the darkness.

A moment later, a rumble came from a nearby bush and the cow lumbered over. Her rash was now a shade bluer.

Upstairs, Milena squeezed out all the tubes from the chemist's into the bathtub. It looked like it was overflowing with thick white whipped cream. Semi-Skimmed jumped in, splattering gunk all round the walls.

'We've got to come up with a new plan,' Milena said. 'Hefty's a tougher opponent than I thought.'

Semi-Skimmed found the toilet brush, which Milena had hidden away, and was now scrubbing her back with it.

Her horns seemed lower than usual, even though she was defiantly crooning something to herself. Milena could make out a few words – 'Run along little moo-cow, the sky's getting dark now ...' – but she didn't recognise the song.

Milena continued: 'Maybe you could learn to parachute for your new talent act, or something flash like that? We've got to find a new training ground at least. Hefty's gang knows where our current one is.'

'Hey,' Semi-Skimmed said. 'Is this cream supposed to make your skin turn green?'

Milena looked at the cow. She saw that her muzzle was covered in a pale bluish lather, but underneath Semi-Skimmed was bright, traffic-light GREEN. Greener than a Granny Smith apple, old cheese or the house at the end of their street. In other words, REALLY GREEN, like spinach from outer space, or algae.

'How come you've gone *green?*' Milena shrieked, then remembered her mum asleep downstairs and whispered in a hoarse voice, 'You're GREEN!' As soon as she said that, she realised it was a pretty

silly thing to say, considering Semi-Skimmed had noticed it herself.

The cow was staring at her hide with the toilet brush in mid-air, totally silent for once.

'It must be due to some kind of chemical reaction,' Milena said. 'Have you got insect repellent on or anything?'

Semi-Skimmed shook her head, then yanked the plug out of the bath and stood there watching the gloop drain away.

'No,' she muttered. 'Just a splash of violet perfume. I don't like the smell of the cowshed.'

Whether it was because of a reaction between the violet perfume and the cream or the wrong phase of the moon, the fact was that Semi-Skimmed was as green as a recycling bin.

'I'll never be able to take part in the Cow Belle Beauty Queen pageant,' she declared, dropping the toilet brush in the bathtub.

'There's nothing wrong with looking like that,' Milena said.

Her dad sometimes used to say that in the old days. It seemed like a very long time ago.

Milena ran some fresh water into the bath, and some pine-scented cleaner, and started scrubbing Semi-Skimmed until the cow mooed in agony. Despite Milena's vigorous scrubbing, the green colour remained. It went a shade more bluish, but it was still distinctly green.

'Maybe we should dye your coat,' Milena ventured, remembering that there was a tube of her mum's old black hair dye in the bathroom cabinet, from the days when she didn't spend all her time lying on the sofa with a pair of woollen socks on.

Semi-Skimmed shook her head. 'I don't want any more problems. I think it would be best to drop the whole thing.'

Milena opened her mouth, but when she saw Semi-Skimmed's expression she closed it again.

44

'I wouldn't have been a match for Hefty. It's foolish to think I'd have any chance of winning,' the cow sniffled.

'You're being defeatist,' Milena snorted. 'Do you intend to let that stupid moo get you down?'

'Yes,' said Semi-Skimmed. 'What do you know about beauty pageants, anyway? You can't even speak properly – you're just a mush-mouth.'

That was a nasty thing to say, but Semi-Skimmed was in a terribly foul mood.

Milena closed her mouth and felt her throat fill with something bitter.

'Put on your own dumb pageant, snot-hoof,' she snapped and stormed out of the bathroom. She threw herself onto her bed and pulled the duvet up over her head. From underneath it, she could hear Semi-Skimmed stumbling out of the bathroom. For a moment, she seemed to pause outside the door to Milena's room, as if she wanted to say something, but then Milena heard her rumble down the stairs.

Who cares if Mum wakes up, Milena thought. *Let her think what she likes about a green Ayrshire barging through the hall covered in soap suds.* Milena wouldn't even care if anyone made fun of Semi-Skimmed. She was a stupid, stuck-up, silage-green, self-important beast, and it was no wonder she didn't have any friends. Who'd want to be around her?

Then again, Milena didn't have any friends in the village herself. But that was completely different. She was afraid what people might say about her lisp. Who would want to play with a girl whose tongue was split in two like a snake's?

The next morning when Mum came in to wake Milena, she was singing the *WestEnders* theme tune as she pulled the curtains open. Milena was gripped by a terrible thought. Her mother had a tendency to be over come with sudden attacks of parental feelings, when she would make Milena eat porridge and ask whether she'd done her homework. No matter how much Milena assured her mum that it was the summer holidays, it didn't help.

If anyone *asked* Milena, she'd say the best mother was one who knew when to leave her child in peace. No chance. Today her mum had woken up in her spot in front of the TV and rung up Lisa Meijer's mum, explaining to her

that Milena needed some new friends. Mum had already been to the flea market and bought a frilly dress, which was too big, for Milena to wear to Lisa's birthday party.

'You'll grow into it!' Mum exclaimed. Milena stiffened. The dress was purple with big red tulips on it and several curtains' worth of pink tulle. Mum always took everything to extremes.

'How about if I wear my black jeans?' Milena suggested.

'And to think I wished for a girl! Well, that's what I got. A pretty girl who wants to dress like some sort of hoodlum.' Mum's lower lip began to tremble, and Milena knew she didn't have any option.

'Sure, it's really pretty.' She sighed.

'It's got puffy sleeves too,' Mum smiled. 'When I

was a little girl I would've sold my own mother to have puffy sleeves. We'll have to take this in a bit, but that won't take long to do.'

'I could sell my mum too,' Milena muttered.

'Whatsh that?' Mum asked, her mouth full of pins.

A couple of hours later Milena found herself in a strange living room. There were kids everywhere she looked. Screeching, noisy, laughing kids. Kids who were all wearing trendy jeans and trainers. In the midst of all the fuss sat a girl wearing a cardboard crown and a cool band T-shirt. Milena had pestered her mum for a T-shirt just like that, but Mum said (AGAIN) that they weren't suitable for little girls. She felt like getting her mum back here and showing her this girl. It seemed there were little girls in the world after all who wore band T-shirts.

Milena stood in the doorway, tugging at the silly lace frills, until some boy ran into her and spilt his Coke over her.

'Oops, sorry,' the boy said without stopping or even glancing at Milena. She shook most of the sugary slop out of her dress and marched over to the girl in the cardboard crown.

'Happy birthday, Litha,' Milena snapped.

Lisa glared at Milena for a good three minutes.

'What's wrong with your mouth?' some boy asked.

'My tongue'th thplit,' Milena said.

Lisa's eyes grew wide. For a moment it looked like they were going to pop right out. Then the corners of her mouth twitched, and Lisa burst out laughing.

'Hey everybody, come and look at this. This cream cake hasn't learnt to speak yet.'

A crowd of children – ravenous, horrible children in rock band T-shirts – circled round Milena and tried to force her mouth open. 'Snake tongue,' they screamed. 'Are you wearing your mum's curtains?'

Milena poked the first boy in the stomach and thrust her knee in the direction of the other until she managed to break free. She rushed off to the loo and locked the door, leaning against it. The raging mob pounded briefly on the door. Then Milena heard an adult's voice, all fake cheerfulness, announcing, 'The fireworks are starting!'

After a brief commotion on the other side of the door there was silence. Milena waited a bit longer. Then she calmed down, took a deep breath and turned to look at herself in the mirror. Mirror-Milena's eyes were dark with fear. She checked in the mirrored cabinet, took out a pair of nail scissors and cut the puffy sleeves off her dress. The boulder that was weighing on her chest eased up a few centimetres. She slashed her skirt with the scissors, tore the rosette off the back of her dress and looked at herself in the mirror. The results weren't too bad. Slightly punk and stylish.

Milena came out of the bathroom. The house was empty – everyone was outside watching the fireworks. She crept into the kitchen, where the table was groaning with birthday food: fancy cakes, cream puffs, little tarts, heaped-up plates of meatballs and little gherkins wrapped in ham, small smoked salmon and cucumber sandwiches.

In the centre of the table was the majestic two-tiered layer cake. A message had been piped onto it in red icing: *Happy birthday, sweet Lisa!* (Sweet? BLEURGH, thought Milena.) The writing was surrounded by a garland of marzipan roses. Lisa's mum must have spent two days creating that iced work of art.

Milena took hold of the edges of the cake plate. Her hands trembled slightly as she carried the cake into the garden. Lisa was standing with her arm around a dark-haired girl. The dark-haired one seemed to whisper something into Lisa's ear, and they both sniggered. Milena saw them glance over towards the boys. She balanced the cake plate on one hand and tapped Lisa on the shoulder with the other. In an instant Lisa's expression changed from surprise to realisation.

She took a step backwards but didn't even have a chance to turn away before Milena smashed the cake into her face. Blobs of cream splatted onto Lisa's jeans. Her dark-haired chum let out a squeal. Milena noticed how the pink rose garland seemed to lend a stylish, artistic touch to Lisa's hair.

'Who's wearing a cream cake now?' Milena asked.

Then she saw the adults approaching. Lisa's mum's face was now a dull purple. Milena got the distinct feeling that the best thing to do was to clear off out of there.

When Milena's mum came to collect her a few hours later, Milena was skulking in some nearby bushes.

'What's happened to your lovely dress?' Mum asked.

'A nuclear bomb,' Milena said. 'It hit as I was rescuing women and children from a burning house.'

'I see,' said Mum. 'That's nice.' Then she looked at Milena for a while and gave her a hug. 'You can tell me if something's wrong,' she said.

'Yeah, sure,' Milena said, looking away. Then she added, 'You've got a sewing machine, haven't you?'

It was as quiet as a mouse in the kitchen. Even the birds outside were silent. Mum was snoring on the sofa. Milena held up her creation and admired her work. She had been sewing all night long. She had drawn up patterns and combined Mum's wetsuit, two pairs of roller skates (from the days when Mum was planning to open a roller-skating café) and an old army tent. The finished results were brilliant.

Milena looked at the kitchen clock and rubbed her cheeks. Six. It was still ridiculously early. Mum wouldn't be up for several hours yet. Milena packed her rucksack and ran out to the field.

The whole meadow by the lake was covered in a mist that hit Milena in the face like a wet towel as she jogged along. Everything looked really different than in the daytime. It felt weird to be out when nobody else was awake yet. Scary. Almost wrong.

Milena stopped to think things over. Mum had said Milena wasn't allowed to be out alone late at night. But technically this was morning. Mum hadn't said she couldn't go out alone EARLY.

56

Milena suddenly had a strange sensation. Almost as if somebody had touched her. She turned round and saw a huge black shape on the hill.

At first she thought it was Semi-Skimmed, but then she realised it was much, MUCH bigger. If Hefty was big, this thing was absolutely enormous. Its flanks were broader than a farm

tractor's. Milena was frozen to the spot. It was as if the creature had materialised from the mist. Its dimensions seemed to reach as far up as the sky.

'It's been up there for a while,' came Semi-Skimmed's voice from behind Milena.

'Semi-Skimmed,' Milena sighed. She had never been so grateful to see any living being.

'Shhh,' the cow said. 'Don't annoy him.'

'Do you know who that is?'

'No,' Semi-Skimmed said. 'But my grandma Bessie told me about them. He's a bison.' The cow let out a long sigh.

'He must have escaped from the bison farm,' Milena concluded. Now she could make out the creature's outline more clearly. It was covered in a shaggy black coat, and its breath steamed up in the chilly morning air. She felt safe with Semi-Skimmed nearby. It's amazing how you don't feel afraid when you're with someone you trust.

The bison snorted. It had noticed them. For a moment it seemed as if it was winking at them. Then it was gone. There was just a shimmer in the mist.

'I know how you can take part in the pageant,' Milena said, digging the things out of her rucksack. For some reason she was whispering. As Milena explained her plan, Semi-Skimmed looked doubtful. But in the end she didn't have much choice.

The Cow Belle Beauty Queen pageant was being held in the field behind the dairy. The place was swarming with local people and tourists who had come to enjoy this rural event. Milena noticed Lisa and her mum among the crowd.

Everywhere there were red-and-white striped booths selling sausages and fizzy drinks, candy-floss and cow-shaped lollipops, liquorice whips and smoked fish. But the best thing of all was the chocolate fountain that had been set up in a prime spot. Shiny, dark melted chocolate bubbled up from its depths. Its crowning glory was a cow moulded in chocolate that strongly resembled Hefty.

Semi-Skimmed nodded towards the fountain

and remarked, 'It's going to be tough competing against that one, isn't it?'

Milena, who had been standing open-mouthed in amazement, quickly closed her mouth and shrugged her shoulders.

'I think Hefty's rump looks pretty broad there,' Milena said, but she was wondering to herself how in the world they were going to get through the competition.

She had never seen so many cows in one place. Dozens of them were jostling on the stage that had been set up in the field. There were black-and-white Friesians, slender spotted ones, black ones, brown ones and pink ones. Massive cows like Hefty and ordinary cows that were absent-mindedly chewing their cud, not taking any particular interest in the hubbub around them.

Hefty stood out from the crowd, even from a distance. Her hide had been brushed until it shone, and her horns gleamed. Snippy and Snooty (that's what Milena called Hefty's two sidekicks in her mind) mooed admiringly at their boss from the edge of the stage. They too had red ribbons round their necks and sunflowers tied round their horns. As soon as Hefty noticed Semi-Skimmed, she howled, 'Look at that one. She's always been ugly, but now she's green as well!'

Snippy and Snooty hooted. The other cows turned to gawp at Milena and Semi-Skimmed. Milena looked at the crowd, but no one was paying any attention to the talking cows. Clearly, adulthood dulled people's senses. They don't want to see anything at all that they're not used to. And preferably with a cup of coffee, the late news on TV and a pair of woollen socks.

'When Skimmy-Dimmy was born,' Hefty bellowed at the top of her voice, 'her mum got such a fright, she produced only sour cream for three whole weeks.'

'Hey!' Snippy (or maybe it was Snooty) noticed. 'How come she's wearing a leotard?'

It was true – Semi-Skimmed's head was the only part of her that was visible. The rest of her body was covered in a tight-fitting bodysuit. Milena had sewn it out of the wetsuit and the tent. The suit was dark green, a shade darker than Semi-Skimmed's muzzle. Milena had stitched large four-leafed clovers onto the garment. (She thought a bit of extra luck wouldn't hurt.) The outfit had helped Semi-Skimmed to recover her self-confidence. Now she walked with her horns held high, wagging her tail.

They lined up with the other cows and their humans. When Milena saw Semi-Skimmed alongside the other cows, she realised Semi-Skimmed had been telling the truth. She really was smaller than the others.

'When's the swimsuit round?' shouted some joker from the audience. Milena recognised him as Farmer Hodge's grown-up son, who people said was a scoundrel. Milena didn't know what that meant, but she suspected it had something to do with drinking beer and playing darts in bars. At least that's what Farmer Hodge's grown-up son did.

Then a man in a pinstriped suit came on stage. He was the town's mayor, and it was obvious he was nervous. He was followed by a perky woman in a posh dress who smiled broadly. Her teeth looked too big and white for the rest of her. The mayor cleared his throat into the microphone and searched for his glasses. The woman in the posh dress snatched the microphone away and welcomed everyone to the Cow Belle Beauty Queen pageant. She said she was a representative of the Milky Ray chocolate factory. She had come here, to the Arctic Bramble district, to find the new cover girl for their top-selling chocolate bar. Hefty – she nodded at the big brown cow – had been a credit to the brand for three years. At this point Hefty, Snippy and Snooty bellowed loudly and blew kisses at the crowd.

The woman wrinkled her brow and raised her voice to continue. She declared the competition open. The judges would be making their choices based on charm, posture and – most important of all – the talent round.

'Have a delicious day, everyone!' the woman in the posh dress squealed, with a smile that made Milena feel as if she were crunching sugar in her teeth.

At the start of the talent round, Milena took out her secret weapon. Semi-Skimmed shuddered when she saw what it was.

'Roller skates,' Milena said. 'I'm absolutely sure there won't be many cows that have thought of these.'

'There's a reason for that,' Semi-Skimmed said, her voice quivering.

'We've got to be quick now,' Milena said as she fastened skates onto each of the cow's four hooves.

'Couldn't we just go home,' Semi-Skimmed grumbled, 'and watch the latest episode of *WestEnders* with your muuuuu ...'

The last word trailed off as Milena gave Semi-Skimmed a push onto the stage. The cow rolled along the stage, bumped into the woman in the posh dress and managed to turn around just

in time to stop herself falling off the edge. The audience was dumbstruck. Everything went silent for a brief moment. The only sound was someone sucking on a lollipop.

Semi-Skimmed was approaching the mayor, but he managed to leap out of the way in the nick of time. After a couple of laps around the stage, Semi-Skimmed got used to the skates and was now looping around more confidently.

The audience snapped out of their astonished silence and began to cheer. That boosted Semi-Skimmed's confidence, and on the next lap she tentatively raised a hoof as she twirled round. The crowd erupted, egging her on.

Milena could see Hefty at the side of the stage, looking even greener than Semi-Skimmed. The woman in the posh dress staggered up and attempted to collect her notecards, which had flown all over the place. She announced: 'There we have contestant number seven, by the name of ...'

'Semi-Skimmed – also known as "Four-Leafed Clover" – Tetra Pak!' Milena shouted. 'The world's only roller-skating cow.' Semi-Skimmed winked, and the front row clapped.

In her excitement at the crowd's reaction, she attempted a pirouette, got her hooves tangled up and flopped onto her belly. The audience roared. They thought the ending was the most brilliant part of the performance.

'It looks like the audience has found their favourite,' the woman in the posh dress said. 'But now the judges will meet to consider their important decision. Meanwhile, our local stars Death Paunch will perform their upbeat hit, "Bloody Tripe".'

A group of bashful farmers, all wearing black leather trousers and black eyeliner, climbed up on stage. Milena recognised her neighbour Masa

69

among the band members. She remembered how many kids in town made fun of Masa because he had a stutter. Now Masa was wearing a leather jacket with a dragon on the back. Masa didn't stutter when he sang.

The band rocked so hard, they were even sweating all over the spectators. Milena figured this was an ideal time to go for an ice cream. She thought Death Paunch sounded better the further away you got from them.

Milena bought a pistachio ice-cream cone for herself and a vanilla one for Semi-Skimmed. (As she was paying, she wondered whether cows actually eat ice cream, but then she saw that there was a big picture of a cow flying against a sky-blue background on the side of the ice-cream stand itself. That HAD to mean that most of their customers were cows.)

Just as she was about to hand Semi-Skimmed her ice cream, she heard a huge commotion in the distance. 'Stop, thief! Someone's stealing the chocolate fountain!'

Still holding the ice creams, Milena turned round to see Farmer Hodge's grown-up son running off with the chocolate fountain under his arm. He had suddenly decided he absolutely had to have a chocolate fountain of his own. The fountain was coating everything in range in chocolate, and all the onlookers just stepped aside. Nobody seemed to want to take action.

Within an instant, Milena had shoved her ice creams into the hands of the person next to her, jumped onto Semi-Skimmed's back and was shouting to the mayor, 'Give us a push. Let's go!'

The mayor didn't hesitate. He gave Semi-Skimmed a big shove on her roller skates. Milena and Semi-Skimmed zoomed along towards the market square and the chocolate fountain thief until – BOOM! They crashed into the man. Chocolate splattered everywhere. Farmer Hodge's grown-up son let out a squeal. He was covered from head to toe in brown gloop and was whimpering in terror. Milena saw something lying on the ground. It was the little statue of Hefty that had been on top of the chocolate fountain – or what remained of it. The chocolate cow had been smashed into so many pieces it looked like a mosaic.

The spectators who had been watching the pageant started to gather round them.

'They've caught the thief!' a little boy shouted.

'That's nothing,' Semi-Skimmed muttered. 'A cow needs to come up with something to do before dinner. It gives you an appetite, as my grandma used to say.' Then she thought for a moment and added, 'Although my poor granny used to go alligator hunting in the sewers, and it always spoiled her appetite. She said they stank.'

Milena stared at Semi-Skimmed for a moment, then spoke to the audience in a clear voice.

'The whole thing was really Semi-Skimmed's idea. She's always playing the hero. The Helsinki police ring her up whenever they're having trouble with murderers.'

'Murderers?' the little boy echoed.

Milena started to feel she might have exaggerated a little too much and hurried to add, 'But only small-scale murderers. The kind that only murder really small people.'

The band had stopped playing, and even more people had gathered round Milena and Semi-Skimmed. The local policeman appeared and clapped his hand on the chocolate thief's shoulder.

'Let's go, Hodge,' said the policeman. 'There's

fish soup on the menu in jail today, with rhubarb cake for dessert.'

'The judges have just returned from their deliberations,' the presenter in the posh dress announced on stage. She wasn't surprised that the spectators had disappeared in the other direction. 'The new Cow Belle Beauty Queen has been chosen. Let's come back to the stage to hear which one of these magnificent animals has won the title.'

'We want the green cow,' shouted Farmer Hodge's grown-up son, whom the constable was leading off to jail.

'The judges have unanimously decided ...' The band sounded a drum roll, and then the presenter continued, 'The winner is someone who's already familiar to us from the past three years – Hefty Hoofington!'

Milena could see Hefty grinning while Snippy and Snooty bellowed. The audience booed, and the presenter looked confused. A small man stretched up to whisper something into her ear, and the woman shook her head.

'This is extraordinary,' Milena heard the woman mutter, but a moment later she had collected herself. 'In a change from last year's competition, this year we have an extra surprise for you.' Hefty's jaw dropped, which Milena thought made her look particularly gormless. 'The chocolate company has decided to launch a brand-new chocolate bar, and we want it to have its very own image on the label. The judges have decided that our Mint Chocolate Truffle bar will feature a cow on the wrapper that looks just like the bar inside: a creature whose colour makes her ideal for this role.'

The crowd roared their approval as Semi-Skimmed scrambled over to the side of the stage. She shook her head and mumbled something. Milena prodded her flank. 'Would Semi-Skimmed

and her young friend please come up on stage?'
said the woman.

'What do you want to say to the audience?'
Milena asked Semi-Skimmed. The cow whispered
something into her ear.

'My friend Semi-Skimmed here would like to say
that, to her, the most important thing isn't winning,
but having a chance to laugh at others. Especially
at Hefty, who's a silly fathead. Also, she wishes

for world peace and less cold milking machines. I understand they feel terrible in the morning.'

The audience applauded.

'I'm not quite sure this speech is really appropriate,' Milena whispered to Semi-Skimmed. 'Shouldn't you be dignified or something?'

'The time to be dignified is when you lose,' Semi-Skimmed said. 'My photo's going to be on a chocolate-bar wrapper!'

And that's exactly what happened. The new Mint Chocolate Truffle bar was such a huge success that people were eating it as far away as Udmurtia. And even though Semi-Skimmed got an unlimited supply of chocolate as part of her prize, her weight never went above 500 kilos. Probably because she was such a keen roller-skater. She even took part in the Olympics – but that's a whole other story.

That day, though, Milena and Semi-Skimmed weren't thinking about the future. The audience crowded round them. Everyone wanted to pat them on the back and praise both of them for their cleverness. Death Paunch started playing, people threw streamers, the whole field was full of people laughing and cows wearing garlands. The woman in the posh dress danced with the mayor, and Milena saw Lisa and her mum cheering in the back row.

Milena leaned over to whisper to Semi-Skimmed: 'Do you think we ought to head home?'

The cow nodded, and so Milena hopped onto Semi-Skimmed's back and they skated down the country road. The sun was setting, and the air was scented with meadowsweet. Milena thought how nice it was to have a friend.

'You know,' Semi-Skimmed said, 'it's nice to win, but it's even nicer to go home when you know there's half a packet of biscuits waiting for you.'

Leena Parkkinen was born in Finland in 1978. Although she comes from a family of gifted storytellers, she really wanted to be a painter. But she did, in the end, by a roundabout route, become a writer. *Cow Belle Beauty Queen* is her first children's book.

Katja Wehner was born in Dessau in Germany in 1976. She studied art and illustration in Halle, Leipzig and Prague. She has been working as a freelance illustrator with various publishers since 2004. She lives in Leipzig with her family.

Ruth Urbom was born in the USA but now lives in England. She translates from Finnish, Swedish and German into English.